The Stone Soup Book of

By the Young Writers of Stone Soup Magazine

Edited by
GERRY MANDEL, WILLIAM RUBEL,
and MICHAEL KING

•

Children's Art Foundation
Santa Cruz, California

The Stone Soup Book
of Poetry

The Stone Soup Book of Poetry
Gerry Mandel, William Rubel, and Michael King, editors

Copyright © 2013 by the Children's Art Foundation

•

Stone Soup Magazine
Children's Art Foundation
P.O. Box 83
Santa Cruz, CA 95063

www.stonesoup.com

•

ISBN: 978-0-89409-029-5

Book design by Jim MacKenzie
Printed in the U.S.A.

Cover illustration by Grace Lackey, age 13

About Stone Soup

Stone Soup, the international magazine of stories, poems, and art by children, is published six times a year out of Santa Cruz, California. Founded in 1973, *Stone Soup* is known for its high editorial and design standards. The editors receive more than 10,000 submissions a year by children ages 8 to 13. Less than one percent of the work received is published. Every story and poem that appears in *Stone Soup* is remarkable, providing a window into the lives, thoughts, and creativity of children.

Stone Soup has published more writing and art by children than any other publisher. With our anthologies, we present some of the magazine's best stories in a new format, one designed to be enjoyed for a long time. Choose your favorite genre, or collect the whole set.

Contents

The Four Seasons

Spring Morning on a Farm

by Levi Crossley, age 12

My black-and-gray rooster crows.
The sound of birds' chatter
filters through the morning.
I open the icy gate
and walk the familiar trail.

A cool, damp haze
swirls around me.
I carry the rusty bucket
filled with a ton of feed;
It pours like sifting sand
into the concrete trough.

Cowbells reverberate
as they prance over the hill.
Stopping beneath my willow tree,
I watch them eat.

I turn around
to head home,
But first I pick the first
Wild buttercup.

Winter Walk

by Dylan Geiger, age 11

A winter walk—
My dog barking by
My side,
Leafless trees
Piled with snow,
Rotten cornstalks
Golden brown,
Cows with frosted fur
Chomping dead grass,
Squirrels feast on
Stored acorns,
Frozen water under
A rusted bridge,
Snow piled in drifts,
As I whistle
Trucks pass.

Firefly Sky

by Jennifer Hu, age 13

The fields are a wonder in summertime:
Midnight black like the sky,
With twinkling lights like stars.

What are those lights?
Hundreds of fireflies flittering about,
Tiny and so nimble.
Their lights shine on and off,
Making the field like shiny sequins,
Like moonshine dancing off the sea.

I run out into the field,
The half-grown wheat scratching my legs,
The ground soft and damp,
The air humid and fresh.

The fireflies dart away from me,
Intimidated by my presence,
But I don't mind.
I watch them from a distance.

They float above the wheat,
Like bright candles in the field.
Glancing up at the heavens,
I see the stars,
Bright candles in the sky.

This is the moment
When Heaven and Earth meet:
The stars in the sky are the stars on the ground.

How strange it seems
That something as small as fireflies
Can bring these two vast kingdoms
Together as one.

Autumn

by Gabriel Wainio-Théberge, age 12

We see autumn
As a blaze
Of red leaves, falling leaf-shaped embers
From the branch-lined sky,
A blaze
Of squirrels rushing,
Geese hurrying, of motion,
A blaze
Of jack-o'-lanterns.

But around the jack-o'-lanterns falls the night,
Advancing slowly through the days,
A black cat stalking the now mouse-weak sun.
Northern winds come
Hand in hand with warm zephyrs
Above the autumn's thin skin of fire,
Waltzing around each other;
Summer to winter and back
While below,
Frost turns soil to stone,
For hardy autumn-leaf mushrooms to stand brittle
Like Medusa's stare.

The Stone Soup Book

Winter

by Riley Grace Carlson, age 9

I walk through the silent pasture to the tree swing.
I sit down and start to swing.
I close my eyes and fall into a silent sleep.
When I open my eyes I see the ground is littered
with leaves, acorns and plants of all kinds.
I sit listening to the wind roar.
I am not troubled.
I just sit there
watching
waiting.

There Was a Blizzard

by Alice Provost Simmons, age 10

Blizzard
white snow
twirling
dancing like
another
kind of ballerina.
I see a girl
she is white—
seeing something
I can't see—
a white hawk
circling

Choir of Autumn's End

by Gabriel Wainio-Théberge, age 12

Listen! Is that the calling of the hounds,
The hounds returning?
What wavering desolate horn is this that sounds,
So much like the wild hunt's baying?
A trembling weary choir of voices
From the chilly gray air.
And they come, then,
From behind the old, mound-like gray hill,
A long-necked mourning choir on wings,
Late geese.
    We are the last
Honks their song
        And should have listened to the wind's warnings.
        Now autumn is ended
        And winter's wingbeats ruffle our tails

Early Spring

by Ava Alexander, age 11

The ice and snow are almost melted,
Winter's biting cold has mellowed,
Mountains brown and bare for so long,
Show an almost imperceptible haze of green.
The sky is the delicate shade of thrushes' eggs
Soon to be laid in a nest of mud and twigs.
A mole furrows the earth's brow with his tunneling,
Cautious tongues of green make their way
Through last autumn's leaves into the balmy air.
The first robin pecks at the newly softened ground,
And drags an unwilling worm into the light.

Winter

by Danica Lee, age 12

The flowers call
Their last farewell
To the woods
As winter comes
To wilt their petals.

The snow falls
Upon brown leaves
Fallen on the roofs
Of houses strung
With sparkling lights.

The crisp air
And glittering frost
The little puffs of breath
And mugs of steamy tea
Only come in winter.

Thirteen Ways to Look at Autumn

by Kelly Dai, age 12

The smell of gingersnaps,
apple cider,
and pumpkin pie
wafting through the air
in delicate swirls
arm in arm with the colorful wind.

The shy sun
poking through
the wooden arms
of a lamenting willow.

Golden drops
of warm sunshine
strewn across the yards
of piled leaves and blades of thin grass.

Quietly,
almost silently,
the bitter wind and its long fingers
pull and wrench at the crackling leaves.

The sighs
of schoolchildren
accompanying the morning fog
on the dawn of the first day.

The clouds overhead
as gray and lumpy
as my grandma's oatmeal.

A flock of geese, united in song,
fly south for the winter.

Shadows trace the geese's dark feathers
against the flames of dusk.
As I watch them fly
the roar of the ocean drowns out my bellow:
Why must you depart?

A dove and a nightingale
cooing along
with the caws of a raven
upon the calling of Hallows' Eve.

Pumpkins and jack-o'-lanterns
with wicked smiles
glaring at you from doorsteps.

The sweet taste of pumpkin pie
dancing upon your tongue.

I do not know which to prefer,
the beauty of contrast
or the beauty of harmony.
The last green leaf
or the vicinity.

The mountain is sighing.
Autumn must be near.

Leaf of Sunshine

by Laurel Gibson, age 12

The forest is calm,
only an occasional chirp of a bird,
breaks the silence,
the sun is buried in a blanket of clouds,
only a few golden rays escape,
just enough to penetrate the darkness,
cool wind rustles through the trees,
gently swaying their nimble branches,
so peaceful,
one single leaf spirals to the ground,
twirling, spinning,
now upon the brown fallen leaves,
lies one of a brilliant sun-yellow color,
with its bright green smudges,
splattered haphazardly across its surface,
a beautiful sight,
compared to the crumpled leaves surrounding it,
it seems like a precious gem,
it is a bit of sunshine,
on a crisp autumn day.

THE STONE SOUP BOOK

Friends and Family

Peeling Apples

by Katie Ferman, age 12

Carefully, warily,
Sitting with my mom at the kitchen table.
She peels quickly: in a few swift moments
One twisted apple peel sits on the cutting board.
I try to copy her, but no—
The knife slips and
Cuts off a small chip of the red peel.
Trying again, I get lost in the smell of the ripening fruit
(Sweet, almost sickly sweet),
Filling the room with a scent like my grandma's house.
And I start to remember the first time
The first time I had *her* apple pie—
I wrinkled my nose and said, "Too sweet!"
(Now it's my favorite dessert.)
The first time I buttoned up my coat
To keep out the cold on an October day,
The first time I read a book
To my mother in broken, unsteady words,
The first time I tied my shoe
After hours of torture and trial—
And as I think of this,
I barely notice the one, perfect apple peel
Sitting on the cutting board in front of me.

Ghost Park

by Sariel Hana Friedman, age 9

Swaying wooden swings
Whisper to each other
The wind blows dry leaves,
Scattering messages across the park.
The white, lacy blur
Of a girl
Polished black boots drum along stone paths
As the boy calls out her name.
"Come back, Margaret!
I didn't mean it!
Come back!"

Tickle Me Pink

by Marissa Bergman, age 12

Buzz!
The familiar sounds of bees pierce my ears
As I lay on the dewy morning grass.
Sprawled next to me is Tessa,
My younger sister,
Doodling with her favorite crayon.
"Tickle Me Pink,
Isn't that a funny name?" I ask.
Squish!
I roll over to hear her reply, and
Stubbles of the freshly mowed grass stick to my back.
Giving me her naïve face she answers,
"What color is your heart?"
Not wanting to confuse the toddler,
I flop against the pole of the basketball hoop with a
Thud!
"What color is spring?"
Tessa persists.

I was too old for her childish games,
"I don't know, now hurry up it's at least
1000 degrees out!"
The grass squelches as she stumbles towards me,
Waving her drawing like a trophy.
She sticks it in my face, and I see her masterpiece:
A picture of her and me,
Lying together in the grass
On a warm spring day.
"Your heart is pink,"
She points to my chest in the drawing,
"And so is spring."
She points to the grass, sky, and flowers.
And at that moment, my Tickle-Me-Pink heart
Is a blossoming bud.

Homesick

by Soujourner Salil Ahebee, age 10

Leaving my dear country
made me sad, made me miss
all that was worth remembering
the food like *foutou*
the food like *attieke*
the food like *aloko*.

Leaving my African country
made me mourn, made me long for
the people like the Baoule
the people like the Senefou
the people like the Dan.

Leaving Cote d'Ivoire
made me sour, made me cry for
the places like Grand Bassam
the places like my grandfather's village—N'Gattadolikro
the places like Abidjan.

Leaving Papa
resting in his grave
made me dispirited, made me despairing.
I miss him
Listening to Louis Armstrong,
reading the poetry of Leopold Senghor,
calling me his *cherie.*

Sailing

by Claudia Celovsky, age 13

The wind caresses my hair
As I grasp the tiller,
The direction of the sail in my hands.
I watch the dazzling turquoise water
Splash up against the boat,
And glance up at my grandma's magnificent face.
"Am I doing OK?"
She answers with a smile and a wink.
I feel so good,
With the seagulls flying all around me,
And the warm summer sunshine
Beating on my bare back.
I feel so good,
With wonder flying all around me
And the warm love of my grandma
Beating in my soul.

For Grandma

by Sayre White, age 13

You drank
hot water
from a chipped mug.
It was so boiling,
that it would have scalded
my tongue.
But you loved it.
I loved the Eggo waffles
that I've never
had without you;
for me they are only
there
in your warm house,
with the rain
pouring
behind the large window,
as it often does
in Olympia.

I remember your soft
freckled hands,
the skin loose and wrinkled,
but still strong,
patiently untangling

my wet hair
with that purple
comb I loved,
as we looked
at Ranger Rick magazines,
and pictures
of Mom's diving days.
You answered
my millions of questions,
and read me
thousands of books
in your rich voice,
on that green plaid couch,
that has since been moved
from your house to mine.

I curled in your lap
and your loud laugh
shook your large frame
along with my small one,
making me giggle
and fold myself deeper
into your well-cushioned arms
until I could feel
your heart against my
wiry back.
I didn't know then,
that someday soon
that heart would fail.

I wish you could see
me now,
Grandma,
see my life
and how I've grown.
I want to show you
the work that I've done,
and together
we could read the poetry
that I've come to love.
But you were gone
too soon.
Gone before
I could say
goodbye,
gone before
you could truly see
the granddaughter
you barely knew.

Mi Abuela

by Anna Lueck, age 12

We sat
As it rained and drenched the thirsty soil
We sat
And laughed and talked and drank tea
Seventy-seven years apart
But closer than a mother and daughter
We exchanged simple words
Mine so young, so naive
Hers wise and old and perfect
I scratched the head of her dog
I dreamed
The dog was my brother and she was my mother
But the dream never came true
She was *mi abuela,* my grandmother
Her hands were as crinkled and dry
As the books she so often gave me
Her body was weak
But her heart was still strong
Or so I thought

THE STONE SOUP BOOK

The day I became old
I learned
of how she lost her will to live
of how she lay there
willing death to take her
I screamed and cursed the earth
And my world clattered down around me
Instead of laughing, now I cried
Why oh why did she want to die?
I cried
Like the rain that covered us
Seemingly so long ago.

The Beginning

by Devorah Malka Reisner, age 12

I watch them
Each face unknown
Their eyes move back and forth
I walk to my desk
In the corner, alone
The teacher begins
I sit there
Watching
Each face wondering
Whispering
Who is she?
As if I'm not there
I glance up
At the girl in front
I see a smile appear
And she laughs
Quietly
Pointing at me
My face burns crimson
I stare down
At my desk

Out of the corner of my eye
I see
Someone toss
A paper
On my desk
I grab it, and read
"Don't mind her," it says,
"She's just being unkind,
Welcome to school"
I look at her
A quiet, red-haired girl
She smiles at me
And I know
I've found a friend.

Happiness in the Johnson Family

by Colin Johnson, age 11

I smell butter cookies, hot chocolate and the stickiness of sleep
As we gallop up the stairs to the family room
My brother jumping up and down beside me
Like a monkey in his tree-green plaid pajamas
The tree is glowing like a pyramid of radium
And the presents, mysterious cubes and ovals
    wrapped in slippery wax wrapping paper
The color of fluffy foamy whipped cream
I hope to get a new skateboard or a surfboard
Or any kind of board that moves
I imagine tearing through the boxes to discover
    the treasure within
We stare at our thumbs as we wait as impatiently
    as dogs about to be fed
For my parents to wake up so we can open presents
But we only hear our dad snoring
As loud as the howl of the wind on a crisp, cold winter night
But then we turn around and see our rumply tousled parents
    in the pine-scented hallway
"You can open your presents now," they say
With smiles as wide as two slivers of the moon
"Finally!" my brother and I shout as we rush towards the pile
    of mysterious presents

In the boxes I find root-beer-scented surf wax
A black leash to hold me to my surfboard
    and my surfboard to me
And foamy grip tape to help me from slipping off the board
And as I hear my mom's graceful laughter
As she watches my brother bounce around the living room
With a ribbon tied around his legs and arms
    as if he were a present
I feel cozy in a blanket of happiness and love

Someone Absolutely New

by Imani Apostol, age 11

A dull, cloudy morning,
On the couch with my parents,
Cozy, like the three little bears.

My dad holds the camera,
…Why?
An unexpected turn in the lethargic morning conversation

My dad tells me to look at some papers,
Confused and unsure,
Why are they meant for me to read?

All the words on the paper were blocked out,
Except for one—like a lighthouse, flashing news…
PREGNANT

My legs jump in the air,
My feet tap out the sound of joy.
Then I know what the camera is for.

These new and different feelings and thoughts
Crowd my head
Like a crowded pack of people at the Macy's Thanksgiving
Day Parade.

I would have to take care of someone
Small, gentle, and fragile like a feather.
What to do, what to do?

This new baby—new person in my life
Will change the way I think of others,
And will change the way I care for others.

A baby brother? A baby sister?
Someone I am excited about,
Someone I'm looking forward to—someone absolutely new.

Frisbee

by Laura Dzubay, age 11

I curl my cold fingers
Around the yellow Frisbee
Coil my arm back
Dip it low, flex my wrist,
Release.
It sails smoothly through the air
Floats gently above my father's head
And then
The wind carries it slowly
Into his waiting hands
He smiles and tosses it
Back into the wind
I am prepared
My arms are open, ready
As his were
To grasp it, to hold it in my clutches
But instead
The wind takes it,
Swoops it, low and high
Suddenly
I am snatching air,
And the Frisbee lands
Softly in the grass,
Wet with mud

I pick it up
Bend low,
Step forward,
Let go.
Dad leaps
With a ballerina's grace
His hands clasp
Around its plastic yellow body
Our eyes lock
He nods, I nod,
A mental understanding
Then it's whizzing through the air
A bright, lemon-colored streak against the violet sunset.
I push off the ground
My feet lift from the grass
I reach for the sky,
Palm open
Instinctively
My hands snap shut
Like the pincers of a crab on the beach
And suddenly it is there
I am holding it
Thud.
My sneakers meet the ground

And I am thrusting it into the air
A triumph
He smiles
I smile
The yellow disk
Is in my hand
We smile
We nod
Go home
Now we are done here.

A New Brother

by Ryan Sparks, age 12

There he was
Such a tiny person
I looked at him
Sleeping peacefully

Suddenly his eyes open
Brand new brown eyes
Staring at me
Blinking and adjusting his eyes to a new experience
Light

His mind consuming
New thoughts
New faces
New world
New everything
He is a new person

THE STONE SOUP BOOK

Animals

The Redwing Blackbird Sings

by Nina Wilson, age 10

In the morning
I wake up
At six-fifteen
Much too early
Hair is combed
Teeth are brushed
Breakfast is had
One day being like another
But
On my way to the bus stop
A redwing blackbird sings
Doo-Dee-OO!
Time stops
But my feet still move
It is March
The air has a fresh rainy smell
The redwing blackbird
Sings again
Doo-Dee-OO!
I am at the bus stop
The bus pulls up
And time starts again

The Dancer

by Anna Preston, age 12

Behind the curtain of rain
The Dancer awaits
Her slick, muscular legs tensing, preparing,
Wide eyes darting, searching.
Suddenly, with all grace, she leaps through the air.
Flying, Soaring,
She lands with flawless balance
Just in time to shoot her slender tongue into the air
For dinner.
The frog on her lily pad.

Puppy

by Emina S. Sonnad, age 12

The little brown dog
huddled up against me
breathes deeply
knowing he is safe.

Crickets chirp outside
an owl hoots
frogs croak
but he sleeps through this
snoring on my lap.

His body is so warm
with each slow breath he heaves
his body pushes against mine
and he knows
that I am still with him.

But as my body stays
with the dog
reassuring him
that all is well
my thoughts travel
and I think back to our
first day together.

He barked at every neighbor
jumped on the table
ate all our good food
chewed up the couch.
No one understood
why we kept him.

But I do now.

His paws are tucked in
his snores are little whistles
he is deep in sleep.
He is completely at ease
peaceful
because he knows I am with him
holding him
keeping him safe and warm.

Where would this little brown dog be
without me?
And where would I be
without him?

He stirs sleepily
and I hug him close
his head drops down
resting in my lap.

And our breathing is now
synchronized.

Like the chirping
of the crickets

I am a Golden Trout

by Colin Johnson, age 11

The sound of silence shatters
When a buzzing fly splashes into a cool freshwater lake
The water, like liquid tourmaline, ripples to kiss
    the sun-bleached shore
I wait for a delicious, squishy fly to plop into
    striking range
Anxious yet excited
Each time is as thrilling as the first
I strike like a ravenous eagle
WHAM!
I clamp the sweet, juicy fly between my jaws
    like a wrench
GULP!
What a luscious fly!
I descend into the liquid silk water
To snooze in my blanket of warm earthy mud

The Opposite Direction

by Benjamin Firsick, age 11

The icy November breeze
Chilled my neck, as muggy
Gray clouds hid the brilliant sun.

Laying my rake down, giving it a rest
From clawing the leaves into a pile,
When the desperate cries of wood thrushes
came to my ears.

The enormous amount of birds made me suck in the crisp air.
I exclaimed, "Wow. You don't see that every day!"

The birds made dips and circular movements,
that were fluent and organized. As the huge swarm flew towards
their destination, one small speck of a bird
    left the pack and
flew in the opposite direction.

The caws and cries of the huge group echoed off
into the early morning sky.
The shrieks and hisses of the hawks greeted them
    as they flew into
Costa Rica and pierced through every heart
    of the wood thrushes.

A living nightmare for the inky black-eared
        wood thrushes,
A temporary amusement for the hungry hawks.

Hawks dived down on their prey like hail on ants.
Wood thrushes scattered frantically
        beating their wings up and
down searching for any means of escape.
Razor-sharp talons and hooked beaks glinted in dawn's
        early light.

The wood thrushes scrambled to and fro—
        "Where to go!"
One small speck of a bird led the others
        out of the jungle, making
swerves and dips as the hawks stopped
        their vicious assault.

They had a joyful reunion with the one daring bird
        that made a
solo flight—and eventually led the others out of
        the hawks' sharp grasp.

The Loss of a Leaf

by Peter Satterthwaite, age 13

It was a picturesque day at a pond,
The glassy water gently undulated,
Transforming turtles to twigs.
The swans slowly carved their way forward,
The paddleboats hypnotically
Slap slap slapped.

But no day is perfect for everyone,
Like the coming of fall,
For betwixt the lily pads,
A swan lay
Dead,
Its head limp at its side.

Two deceivingly collected swans swam up,
Their wings arched over their backs.
One of the mourners swam up and went
    from calm and collected
To aggressive and emotional.
It began biting the neck of the dead swan,
    wings pumping, causing a great ruckus.
Was it cannibalizing or freeing the other swan
    from its eternal sleep?

That swan will be denied so much,
Days like today,
Cygnets,
And the late summer water relaxing away troubles.

Was it dead from natural causes, or man-made ones?
Could it have been saved?

So many questions,
Like the water in the clouds,
So much stress and more worry than bugs
	in a humid summer's night.
All from
The loss of a leaf.

The Brown-and-White Tabby

by Mia Ba-Lu Hildebrandt, age 12

I leave for school,
Strolling with my mother.
My tiny pink backpack is slung over my shoulder.
It is a crisp, autumn day.
All the leaves
Changing pigments.
My mother
Constantly reminding me to
Walk faster.
To keep up with her,
I drag my little feet along.
Into the dirt they go...
And there! As I round the next corner,
I hear a faint tinkling.
It's not my imagination. I spin around
And lay my eyes on it!
Yes! It's a brown-and-white tabby!
Mother scolds, "Mia, keep walking.
You get so distracted over little things in life."

As our walk progresses,
I still hear the tinkling, sweet little bells ringing
    from the kitty's neck.
Every few seconds I turn my head around,
Checking to see if the tabby is still there,
And it is.
As I check back one last time, my mother says,
"Mia, we're here at Linden. Hurry up,
Or you'll be late!"
"Bye, kitty!
See you tomorrow!"

The Wolf

by Caley Scheppegrell, age 13

I sit on the porch
The dark woods around me
Insects chirping
And listen
To the distant sounds of the party
Inside.

It is a party thrown for me,
By my parents.
A party I didn't want—
Strangers crowding into our little house
People I don't know
Pinching my cheeks
Muttering lies about
"How she's grown!"

I escape to the woods
Fleeing the lights
And the cheerful, pointless chatter
And crouch in a dark clearing
Reveling in the silence
And the dark.

A flash of movement
And a wolf creeps into the clearing
I freeze in fear
Breath making tiny white puffs in the air
Terrified to move
Terrified to stay still.

The slim, strong, deadly animal
Looks at me
Dark, intelligent eyes.
Like my own.
We stare in silence
Caught in the spell of the winter woods.

Then I whisper,
"You're alone, too?"
The beautiful, elegant head
Seems to dip in a nod
And then the wolf
Proud, fierce, and yet gentle,
Turns and vanishes into the shadows.

I walk slowly back to the house
Returning to my party
Where I wasn't missed.
Before I go inside
I turn
For one last look.
Hoping somehow
She had come to say goodbye.

The trees are still and empty.
Disappointed, I reach for the door
And then stop—
A sound from the forest.

A long, lonely howl.
It starts out rough
But spirals up into a sweet, sorrowful note
That sounds like tears
And ends.

I think of the wolf
Alone in the forest.
I face the trees and whisper,
"Me too."

The Whale

by Isaac Goodman, age 9

The whale gently glides across the surface
his sad, long, moaning music enchants all he meets
to rejoice the sound would be a wronging
for he is sad, lonely, cold
his sister has just lost her life
and the two-legged ones did it
an empty feeling embraces his head
and the wind drowns out his thoughts
as he peacefully swims away

Nighttime

Into the Night

by Eliza Putnam, age 13

Loud chirping surrounds the house.
It is hard to concentrate on anything else,
While the wood frogs and peepers are calling.
Silently, I put down my book,
    and slide away from my chair.
I lean out of the window, seeing nothing,
But feeling something in the air.
The stars are shining brightly.
I cannot see the tiny creatures,
But their voices are calling, calling,
Begging to be heard.
Suddenly, I am through the window
And into the night.
Sitting on the porch roof,
Letting the chirps and peeps envelop me.
The tiny animals of the swamp are calling, calling,
We are alive.

Moonbeams

by Lauren MacGuidwin, age 12

Big and bright
It stood and watched me.
Shattering as I
Skipped stones
Across the surface
Of the
Solid lake,
The ripples spread its
Perfect whiteness.
Silent but bold.
It moved the ocean waters.
It was howled at by the
Wolf,
Enraged by loneliness.
It lit the path of the
Dead night.
I cup the cool, crisp
Water in my hands and
Splash them on my face.
The drops
Capture its rays
And I am splashed
With moonbeams.

Watching

by Laine Bruzek, age 12

I lie on the grass,
My back on the soft earth,
Wind quietly whistling
Through the tall oak behind me
I watch the sky
And as the clock spins
The sky does also,
The clouds passing through
On their way
To the rest of the world
Gently waving their shape-shifting fingers
And floating away
The sun finishes its continual arch
And shows off its silent brilliance as it
Prepares to slip below the horizon
Its light piecing the rainbow on the blue canvas sky
Like an enormous jigsaw that
Just like the clouds
Shifts every day, then fades to blue

A deep, restful blue held back by the tiny pinpoint stars
That emerge from their day of sleep
And wink at the last of the sun
Then turn respectfully again towards the moon
Their moon.
Their hushed lullaby a soft glimmer
As the moon holds itself with such posture,
Such presence.
Carrying out its midnight duty.
And as I breathe it in, I feel like one of them.
Goodnight, I whisper to them.
And I truly am happy to be alive.

Joys of the Night

by Katie Ferman, age 13

At first glance, only shadows
Only wisps of black knitted into
The patchwork quilt of springy turf
Where magic warms the notes of moon's music,
Light playing upon scruffy T-shirt and shorts,
Hair swirling, legs
Twirling,
Hoping to gather treasure in her net
Then out of dark and fresh-lain night:
A tiny little bead of light
Up, up swoops the net with arms raised high
And the balls of bare feet jump to meet
The moon
And lo, the little flickerin' thing
Is caught up in the net
And she reaches balled fist in eagerly,
Band-Aids patching up hurts of yesterday,
And tiny, warty fingers fix themselves round their catch,
But, try as she will to cut off its light,
Clasping both hands round the firefly,
She cannot kill the hope of the creature
That has been caught before,

And the giggles, the attempts to close in
　　the beams of yellow
Only amuse the moon
For what would parents know of such
　　important matters?

And as she releases the firefly's light
It sails back off into the night.

One Night in Autumn

by Rhiannon Grodnik, age 12

The wind
Is blowing strongly into my face.
It feels good.
I close my eyes and lie back
In the wet grass.

It is dark out and everyone else is sleeping.
Everyone but me.
It's a nice feeling, being alone
Out here.

Tick-tock.
I hear the sounds of my watch,
Every second, every minute.
Why does my watch have to remind
Me of the time passing?
It was nice to forget
About time.

Always people are so busy,
They never have time to think
About who they are
And who they want to be.

Am I really here, all alone, so close to my home,
Yet so far?
Is this a dream?
Everything that happened and everything
    that will happen
Rides away on the wind—
Up, up it goes
Past the moon and into infinity.

Dawn creeps in on me and I quietly let myself
In through the back door.
I tiptoe up the stairs into my bedroom—
Like a burglar in my own house.

Safe in my bed again,
I pretend I'm sleeping.
No one will ever guess where I was that autumn night—
But I will never forget it.

Empty Spotlight

by Cora W. Bucher, age 13

Does anything exist at this hour,
when my footsteps crash,
and my breathing screams?
When every slight movement I make,
Feels like a leap?
When I'm all alone,
my house is quiet.
Outside the streetlights blur,
and twist themselves into shapes that
spotlight on the patch of gravel,
that's empty.
No one is there,
to stand in that spotlight,
and listen to the applause,
of the grass, blowing
in the wind.
And I am inside,
looking out,
at an empty place,
that I wish were
mine.

Night in the Woods

by Amanda Johnson, age 13

Smoke rising
Into the dark sky
Crickets chirp
And a twig snaps
Warm air presses against me
And a cold wind
Blows behind my back
The fire crackles
And Mother laughs
As my marshmallow
Blows up in flames
Then it is bedtime
Crawl into the tent
The air is cold
But inside the sleeping bag
It is warm
The glow of the fire
Shines through the tent
As a stick cracks
And I drift asleep

Sunset

by Rhiannon Grodnik, age 11

I watch the sun melting like butter into the calm swirl
    of waves and foam
It glides down, a flying ballerina
In the far end of my vision, I can see shimmering
    stars glistening:
City lights
I look deeply into the vast universe below,
    a world of its own,
And see reflections
Somewhere, I can be sure, someone else is beholding
    the same image.
And watching the same moon run like a track star into
    the waiting sky,
Her finish line
I hear the buzz of voice and wind and sea,
    blended to perfection
I breathe the deep night air in deeply and regard
    the infinite sky,

Ever changing like the world around me
And in that short moment of life, everything is silent
I can remember none of my past, and can think not
    of my future
I can hear no buzz, only the rhythmic sounds of
    my heart and my breath
I feel I am alone on this earth, alone with the stars and
    the moon and the wind
Alone with only one song to listen to:
The song of peace that has been heard by many before,
And will be for many to come
And then it all disappears:
The aloneness
The light
San Francisco,
Into darkness

Down at the Dock

by Rebecca Mitkus Wishnie, age 10

Down at the dock
when all is dark,
my footsteps clang
and echo
on the metal
corridor
above the ocean.
Filling the near silence,
accompanying the
shhhh
of the waves
and the thud
thump
of the silver
boats
knocking on the
dock.

And the
sssss...
callop
sssss...
callop
of the
white-crested
waves
disintegrating
on the peaceful shoreline.
Look at the
black sky!
White sparks
in the darkness of night,
the kindling of light.

Nature

Dawn

by Sophia Gehrmann, age 13

The gray sky wavers
Between day and night.
A distant train whistle blows
Skimming the solidity of the moment.
Quiet again,
The atmosphere is unreal.
No movement,
Other than the occasional rustle
Of wind stirring leaves.
A brave bird calls out,
Unsettled by the silence.
No reply.
The heavens lighten,
Until finally
The sun appears,
Smiling upon the world.
The birds now begin to sing,
A chorus of relief,
All with the same message:
The day has come.

The Sea

by Wujun Ke, age 13

Standing on a stretch of glossy rocks
lumps of mussel shells
adorned with seaweed
advance forward into my grasp.
Murky greens color the water
in shady reflections,
the thought of wind and shadows
combined.
There is no divider for sky and sea
they are intertwined
like ivy leaves around each other.
For what is not related,
in this cool, salty,
boundary-less place
where the deep comes alive
from bottomless water

The Leaf and the Web

by Taylor Nelsen, age 11

Lines… Veins… Silky Strands…
One red leaf on a green tree,
Swaying all alone in the wind
One red leaf falling through the chilled fall air
Swirling in the twilight.
A busy spider in the early hours of dawn,
Silk webbing falling behind,
Swirling strand, into lines, into web of silk.
Twilight
One red leaf is swirling,
Falling it twirls one more time,
A beauty…
A web with one red leaf
Intertwined in the silky strands.

Meadow

by Julia Lipkis, age 12

There are scattered
wildflowers
wilting among the coarse grass.
Solitary
deer
graze on prickly
stems.
Birds gossip
in the branches
of
dead
oak trees.
Sunlight casts a
dappled
shadow
onto the
hard
dirt.
And the wind
whispers
secrets to me
over the
bent
corn.

But Still It Waits

by Nicholas Bonavolonta, age 12

A tree
Waiting
Standing high, drinking water
Through its mighty roots
Near a river
Shimmering blue
As smooth as glass
It watches the leaves fall
And quickly swept away by the river
Swept far, far away
But still it waits

Its branches blow gently
Back and forth
A fish jumps out of the water
Glistening in the sun
The tree wonders
What it is like underwater?
But still it waits

The tree hears birds flying
Near its branches
Taunting it
By flying far away
And coming back
The tree wants to explore
Wants to see the world around
But still it waits

It is now afternoon
And the tree looks around
It sees the beauty of what is around it
It longs to see what is down the river
Or over the mountain
But still it waits

The Sea's Hug

by Annie Rudisill, age 11

The sea opens its arms to me
Hugging me by pulling me into its deep cool waters
My head goes under
The waves crash overhead
I hug it back
I swim deep
To the bottom
No rush to get air
My feet feel the sandy bottom
I swim back up
To smell the crisp fresh salty breeze pass by me
I see mossy rocks slipping under the waves
Seagulls cry loudly for their friends
I see bright neon-colored sea glass glittering in the sun
I walk onto warm sand
But the sea calls me back to play
I can't resist
I run into its cool hug once again

The Lonely Star

by Cayley Zjak, age 12

The rustle of rough leaves awakens me from my rest
And I gaze up at a dark sky as vast as the sea
And laugh as the stars tumble into my hair
"How green your leaves are!" the stars whisper
    in my hair.
"How bright with happiness you are," I sigh.
"No. The sky is cold and lonely," the stars moan.
"At least the birds don't peck at your arms
and the squirrels don't hide nuts in your armpits."
"But the birds sing to you and the squirrels tickle
    your bark."
"True, I'm lucky to be a tree."
"Alas, my nearest neighbor is ten light-years away."
"But you guide people through the darkness."
"Yes, we do," the stars whisper, their voices tinted
    with new light.
And as a blue jay's soft feathers brush my arms,
I inhale the sharp green sent of pine,
and I laugh

Cape Cod Bay Tide

by Sophie Anne Ruehr, age 11

Our suspicion grows
as the tide rises.
The path is gone
along with the beach,
blocking our way.
The marsh has disappeared,
the sand a new brown,
the sky a pale gray.
Ice chunks linger
in the ever flowing waters.
The bird cries are far out on the bay
where the ice banks end,
where open water lies.
Jump from island to island,
making sure not to get splashed
by the freezing salt water.
Our dog runs out onto the icebergs,
and then comes shivering back
to our heels.

The cold wind blows
and seems to push the tide in.
The trunks of the pines
touch the bank,
inches away from the sea.
The sun hides,
and the hills seem to grow
with the shadows.
The eyes of little crabs
come from holes along the beach,
and scurry to higher ground.
This is high tide.

I Taste the Sky

by Isaac Kamgar, age 11

We fly like falcons over sheets of soft snow
Listening to the distant kinks and grinds of
     steel against rails
The scent of snow cools my mind
And I taste the blueness of the sky

The Storm

by Lincoln Hartnett, age 10

Brilliant splashes of yellow light
Spewing all corners of the earth
With a radiant glow of scarlet

Then darkness
A shield of gray

Then the rains
Pounding relentlessly
On the cold
Damp
Ground

The wind
Slowly growing
With every passing second

A clap of thunder
Vibrating the water-drenched ground

Then peace
The storm retreats.

Pursuit

by Kym Goodsell, age 13

Her pudgy feet ran through the grass
Sparkling in the morning dew
Her footprints left a trail behind her
Impressions on the cold ground

She ran
Her feet stumbling on unfamiliar territory
She tripped and stumbled to the ground
She rose without hesitation and again began her pursuit
Of the beautiful winged creature

Its wings carried it higher
Faster than her little feet could take her
Yet she ran
Willing herself to go faster

She closed the gap
It was nearly in her reach
She sprung from the ground
A single finger brushing a delicate wing
Then it was off and she hit the ground

It fluttered away
Soaring to the sky
While she stayed grounded
Her face misted
Her knees green
But with a smile forming

She accomplished her goal
She touched the butterfly

Silent Story

by Mina Alexandra Oates, age 7

On a cold winter morning
The lake breathes out steam
Like a giant tea kettle.

Two ducks in the middle
As still as a painting.
Why haven't they gone south?

A bird hangs up in the air.
Let's sit on the shore
And soak in the quiet.

Instead, we zoom by
And join in the traffic.

Monolith

by Eden Amital, age 13

Carved, crooked peaks outline themselves against a
Yellowing sky,
Deep crags littered with fertile eggs

Cawing to the firming moon,
We flap between their statuesque
Shoulders, draped in heavy fog
They don't dance

Their shadows do,
Trembling freely outside of the rocks'
    impenetrable cases,
Sharing secrets with the sand,
A peppered canvas,
Which formed when
The smeary stars
Cracked and crumbled

We gulls fly,
The stones too stiff
To crane back their necks
And see us,
Swooping, whooping,
Following an invisible course
Sliced into the sky

Echoes

by Alyssa Fowers, age 13

slate
the word itself
is harsh
final
the sound
of rock-on-rock
metal-on-metal
an avalanche's
moaning shriek.

but the stone itself
breathes.
lives.
shadows play

under its skin
the echoes resting
on its surface
palest blue
frailest pink
a whisper
a murmur
a pinch of cloud
twining about
muted rainbows
a breath of sunset
rising
amid a silver sky

My Landlord on an August Morning

by Alyssum Quaglia, age 12

My landlord wakes to a dawn
where everything is silent, and even the trees
still linger in the unconsciousness of night.
Dewy grass dampens his shoes
as he strolls out over to his most used patch of land:
the garden. The smells are soft and fresh
and the rain's clear drops
from the night before
are a blanket strung with pearls,
that drape over the green leaves of lettuce
as he walks over to tend them.

A cricket sounds in the strawberries,
awakening the rustle of wings,
but the bird passes over,
gliding on an invisible thread
through the air.

My landlord's hands,
rough, yet tender in his work,
soften the moist earth
at the roots of the unwanted,
allowing him to
pull them up,
and let his green, leafy children

live on.

For No One

by Mara Schiffhauer, age 12

I watch her
From the garden
A baby girl
Wobbling around, like a buoy
On a choppy ocean,
Batting playfully
At her rainbow of toys,
Her blue eyes,
Darting around the room.
Her mother softly coos,
"So big,"
With a pearly smile
Drifting gently up her face.
The baby shoots
Her tiny fingers
Towards the heavens.
The mother,
Clapping and cheering,
Tells everyone.

But when I
Was a sprout,
Nestled warm
In my cocoon of soil,
Like the jelly encased
In a fluffy doughnut,
Soaking up the nutrients,
Readying for my awakening,
The thunder boomed to me,
"So big!"
With its blinding smile
Shooting straight to the ground.
I sprawled out
My verdant fingers
And rocketed to the sky,
My tiny heart full
Of pure pride;
All the creatures in the forest
Saw me,
But they told
No one.

THE STONE SOUP BOOK

Reflections

Hanging the Laundry

by Isabel Sutter, age 12

Sunlight
Dapples the long white laundry line.
Holding the plastic basket
On my sore hip
I lift a battered, hand-knitted
Cream-colored dishcloth
And hang it on the line.
A monarch butterfly flits about the yard
And a daring mourning dove
Tries to settle herself
On the laundry line.
I watch the line
Swaying in the cool breeze.
The sun dances across
The towels
And splatters them with color
Like an artist's palette
Dotted with creamy-yellow paint.
Hanging the last towel
I step back to survey my work.

Haven

by Misha Kydd, age 12

Soft, quiet, a blanket of books,
Turn left, left again, up the stairs,
Feet finding the usual route.
Passing comrades, enclosed in words,
To the end of the row, near the window,
The chair, my haven,
Of books.
I don't notice when it grows dark,
Outside,
I don't look up from the knights,
And dragons, and swords, and horses.
The problems in this world are easier,
To face than the ones in
Mine.

White

by Dylan Sherman, age 10

White is the color of
Beautiful

Like a dove
Soaring over a forgotten mountain lake
Snow
Blanketing the landscape
In a soft white
Paradise
Essence of pine

Like a cello's music
Sweeping the night
Alone
But that makes it even more
Serene

Like a white sail
Rising up a mast
Against a coral blue sea
Waving about
Taking
You there

Like a patch
Of white roses
Among the ashes
The start
Of new life

When I Understood

by Malini Gandhi, age 13

New Delhi, India, 2002
Staring wide-eyed out of the car window
I look down at the dusty bodies of children clustered
    below me.
Their hair is streaked with dust and grime
Their skin darkened to a crisp by the intensity of the
    broiling summer sun.
Their writhing hands clutch at the shiny silver metal
    of our car
Grabbing hungrily at the colorful juice boxes
    my parents offer from the windows.

I know I should be enjoying the bustling world
    around me, but somehow I can't.
The road is a blur of color and life;
Vendors shout from their stalls
Advertising a rainbow of colorful fruits and vegetables
Or fine cloth dyed sunset orange, rose pink, indigo.
Sweat clings to their dark skin as they haggle and argue
    with customers passing by
Or just catch up on the latest gossip.

Chickens strut through the crowd like confident butlers;
A cow slowly ambles its way through the people.
Despite the crowd the blasting honks
    of cars' horns sound as they force their way through,
Shiny metal islands in a sea of bodies.

But I am taking in none of this;
My eyes are riveted to the children.
I catch sight of a girl about my age,
Seven,
Her dark hair pulled back in a messy braid,
Clutching the grubby hand of a wriggling two-year-old.
Seeing the look of amazement and longing that fills
    her eyes
As her gaze sweeps over our car
I offer her one of the juice boxes
With trembling fingers.
She grabs it
Immediately handing it to her little sister.

Just watching the little girl inhale the sweet drink
Its contents spilling from her mouth and running
    down her chin like a thousand rivers
I think of all the times I've stormed out of the room
    crying after losing a game of checkers,
Argued with my brother about who had to go first
    for piano lessons,
Made faces when my parents made me eat vegetables.
I can remember those times when my mom got angry,
Yelling, "Don't you understand, there are children
    dying in the world?"
Looking down at the thin, hungry bodies of the children
    surrounding me
At the toddler devouring the juice
At the grateful look the girl gave me
I realized that,
For the first time,
I did understand.

Back Down to Earth

by Jacob Dysart, age 13

The wind is in my hair as I kick with my foot
The rhythm of my wheels on the cracks of the sidewalk
Thu-thump, thu-thump, thu-thump
The curb is coming to meet me at the end of the block
It draws closer and closer
Its short drop seeming like a cliff
I lean back slightly, about to go off
And then it happens
That sweet split-second in which I am flying, untouched
    by worldly problems
Just flying
Then, as my wheels touch down, the entire world
    comes back in a single gust of wind
Thu-thump, thu-thump, thu-thump
Back down to earth on my skateboard

Beating the Storm

by Alec Zollman, age 13

I zoom uphill
Take a cautious turn onto the road
Coasting downhill feels great
Like jumping in the ocean
No pedaling, a cool breeze
Still lurking in my mind
The thought of pushing the limit
To go back uphill
I slowly come across a steep hill
My thighs burn
I am going in slow motion
But it is worth going up this hill
For the thrill of going down the other side
The cool air whips across my shirtless skin
I rocket down the hill

Hill by hill I pedal
Until my body feels like one big wet noodle
A storm cloud approaches
Making it more of a challenge to get to the lake

The air feels like swimming in hot water
I finally reach the last hill
My energy bursts
Like squeezing water from a sponge

I reach the lake
Relief fills my body
First move... JUMP IN
The water is perfect

Riding the Gondola

by Anna Elizabeth Blech, age 12

New York at dusk
When shadowy sun
Rests on skyscrapers
And in the park
In the city
Dragonflies murmur
Birds hum
As the little gondola
Glides across the silver lake
That parts between my fingers
The tenor of cheerful chatter
From the restaurants
The whispered conversations
Of the couples
On their sunset rowboat trips
The swan
Splashing
Preening its feathers

One by one
As night comes to the city that never sleeps
The man on the gondola
Sings in a resounding baritone
"Venite all'agile
Barchetta mia
Santa Lucia
Santa Lucia"
"Come to my
Swift little boat
Santa Lucia
Santa Lucia."

Cubing

by Andrew Lee, age 13

He holds the cube in his hands
The unbreakable puzzle,
Or so they say
Flexing his fingers

He holds it gingerly
Like a trusted friend

The stopwatch beeps
His fingers fly over the cube
Attacking the colors
Orange, green, blue, and whites
Spark through the air
In graceful motions, his fingers

Working like bees
Shift through the layers
Suddenly,
Out of the blue
The cube emerges from his palms

Like a miracle, the cube is whole once again
The stopwatch beeps

And the magic stops

Maui

by Eddie Mansius, age 13

Waves are crashing all around me,
The sun is casting its yellow rays upon the island.
I hear a yell but it is oh so distant:
"Go! Go!"
I turn my head to see a wall rapidly approaching.
I thrash my arms and kick,
But it seems too late for me.
I push up onto the board and stand,
Keeping my balance.
The timing is perfect,
I sail onward to the palms in the distance.
I am flying.
No, I am face down in the sand,
Waves lapping at my feet.
For a moment I think I am dead,
But my board slithers up beside me.
I smile and laugh.
I did it.
I surfed.

Dawn

by Wujun Ke, age 13

The first shaft of luminous light
travels, its speed unthinkable
Over the horizon, through the trees,
And into my open eyes.
Birds hop about, like people,
Trying to find a good
Perch, branch, position
In life. Satisfied, they begin their
Throaty chorusing, declaring
only the best.
Window open, the maple and oak
Scent drifts like it has done
For millions of years, a crisp
Beginning to the significance
Of the day, three hundred and
Sixty-five rotations a year,
Time's luck which decides so much.
As after a rainstorm,
Water has never smelled so sweet.
During the time between dreams
And reality, air has never
Tasted so good.

When I Was Five

by Ashok Kaul, age 11

When I was five, I got out of school.
It was the first day and
I had already made friends.
But none of us knew
what was happening.
I heard a lot of talk about
crash mess fall tall.
Why was everyone talking
about mess fall hit hurt
and tears. Fear.
My mom took me home.
The streets were empty.
I heard fire trucks and police cars.
Then my mom told me.
The two towers were missing.
I was five. It was September 11.
Suddenly, I felt unsure.

The Cool Counter

by Nicholas Wilsdorf, age 12

Mmmm, the man on the bench says as he plunges
a spoon into his mouth.
Aaaah, his wife says as she pulls
out a clean white spoon from her lips.
The woman at the front of the line grins.
A little girl to the left of me is dancing
like a ballerina, with a cup in one hand and a spoon in
    the other.
Ice is shaved into thousands of pieces.
Conversations have no meaning.
I hear an occasional *mmmm* or *aaaah*.
Finally, it is time to make a selection.
Sweet Strawberry?
Wet Watermelon?
Merry Margarita?
Ripe Raspberry?
I know, Gushing Grape.
I watch the ice being poured.
My lips go dry.

The flavors are glazed on,
and my tongue nearly falls off in anticipation
Finally, my cup is full,
and I am bouncing like a wild kangaroo.
The counter girl places it on the cool counter.
I grasp my treat and dig in.
My taste buds take flight.
Cold ice graces my tongue,
as the sweet flavors rush down my throat.
The taste gets better.
Before I know it, my cup is empty.
Yum.

Envelope

by Olivia AscioneD'Elia, age 13

surrounded
every day
by glow-in-the-dark stars
gummed to the ceiling
and photos
like a virus engulfing the walls

images of wooden birds and chlorine-rich summers
cherry blossoms and children in plastic hats
taped mosaic
across plaster

the house
over a century old
with closed-off dumbwaiters
grimy stained glass
tin ceilings sagging
canned antiquity

house under tree bower
turns pink at dusk
mourning doves nest
on the air conditioner crying

night house drowns in dark ink
façade retreating into obscurity
windows glow over the street
where light from passing cars
swims into dark rooms
disappearing into the walls again

The Canal Towpath Near Sand Island on a September Afternoon

by Rory Lipkis, age 9

A solitary autumn leaf rustles on a tree.
Slowly, gracefully it floats down, twirling,
silently meeting the dense dappled shimmer
of still water.

Overhead, distant vees of geese appear.
Their faint raucous cries float on a soft breeze.
Sticks weave around rocks to form
warm tables where turtles sunbathe languidly.
Dragonflies swoop and hover like sylphs
admiring their likenesses in the mirroring water.
Lithe water striders skate across the skin of the canal.
Schools of sinuous minnows flit like brown shadows
below. Salamanders crawl over the slippery logs
submerged under thick algae and creep away.

The green lacewings buzz perpetually among the reeds.
Swamp roses clustered by the bank
sway delicately in clumps of switchgrass.
Mingled jewelweed and loosestrife nod to passersby.
People fish, jog, ride bicycles,
alone or in couples or in families.

I trudge on the dusty path past
a child casting a line into the hazy water.
He pulls a fish flipping and gasping from the murky depths.
The child's father congratulates him,
and the fish's life
slips away.

Soda cans, rusty metal shards, plastic bottles, old tires
are strewn among the brambles.
The transfixing image doubles itself on the water,
distorted here and there by a dead branch hovering low
or a grimy plastic bag caught in weeds at the water's edge.

The placid mirror reflects it all.
The river flows on, around snarls of fallen trees
trailing skeletal gray fingers in the water.
Two boys doubling on a single bike,
     one on the handlebars,
ride by me. Their heads swivel to stare.
They mutter something harsh.
Cars judder over the looming bridge
like distant thunder.

Mismatched

by Pierie Korostoff, age 12

Paperwhites were sagging about the sink.
You could smell fresh air on them
if you got close enough.
Their curtain, white and green,
the only one on the kitchen window
And through it, snow refused to budge.
Odd to have flowers and snow
even if they matched in color.
Except the stems, of course,
they stood out like the green bottle next to the clear glasses,
like the chicken magnet
among those little magnetic words
that never spell what you want.
Words like "bubble"
but not "the" or "and."
Why would I need to write about bubbles?

My toe rubbed against the polished maple rung
of the tall kitchen stool
silent rhythm to the dog's tapping nails,
parents mumbling,
ever-present radio, NPR
or a Cuban CD.
A jumbled soundtrack
to my moment of thinking nothing,
forgetting to check the notes
that came and went,
muddling over the fridge;
my tiny collage.

Mountain

by Emily Riippa, age 13

Pure, dazzling white
Miles of ice
blend with
miles of snow and
snow-covered rock
which can be deadly if you
don't know where to look

A solitary climber
winds
his way up this mountain
stopping only now
and then
to adjust his tinted
snow goggles
This high up
he almost feels ill
overwhelmed by the sheer
altitude of this mountain
which he has come to love
in a way
as his own
the altitude of his moutain
can do this to people—make them feel

so ill that they never make it up
to the summit
but he will
he vows this to
himself

Each step is a mountain
in itself
the snow is quicksand
it wants to drag him
down with every step
he takes
but he fights back
and wins this
battle
thinking only
of the summit
the very top
oh the view from the summit
nothing else is on his mind
not even the ever-diminishing
speed
of his steps

He sees the snow is
ending—could it be
the summit is only
fifty yards away?
He quickens his pace
His struggles are pushed like
mere toys
to the back of his mind
with one last step
a step taken more by
determination and resolve
than by the energy of his
body and his feet

He reaches the summit
and looks down

Ocean Memories

by Eden A. Marish Roehr, age 9

As the notes take me
I try to remember
The ocean
Mom and Dad stand by me
Deeper we go
Jumping big waves
My parents lifting me up to jump
Dolphin fins out in the horizon
Laughing then
Longing now
For the sea to sweep me
Off the ocean floor
As it did a few years ago
If only I could go back
Into childhood memories
See what I did not savor enough
Be there once more
And I go there
As I fall sound asleep
And my dreams carry me back out to sea

CPSIA information can be obtained at www.ICGtesting.com
Printed in the USA
LVOW06s0617181013

357423LV00002B/7/P